observations, the spare poetry a good vehicle for a young man's attempts to articulate the puzzle that is his life."

"Any kid who has struggled to reconcile their identity with the expectations and desires of their parents will find this a familiar but hopeful tale."

More from Nikki Grimes and Wordsong

Ordinary Hazards
Words with Wings
C Is for City

Also by Nikki Grimes

Between the Lines
Bronx Masquerade
Chasing Freedom
Dark Sons
A Dime a Dozen
A Girl Named Mister
Jazmin's Notebook
Kamala Harris: Rooted in Justice
Legacy
One Last Word
Planet Middle School
The Road to Paris
Talkin' About Bessie

NIKKI GRIMES

GARVEY'S CHOICE

WORDSONG

AN IMPRINT OF BOYDS MILLS & KANE

New York

For information about permission to reproduce selections from this book,
please contact permissions@bmkbooks.com.

Wordsong
An imprint of Boyds Mills & Kane, a division of Astra Publishing House
wordsongpoetry.com
Printed in the United States of America

ISBN: 978-1-62979-740-3 (hc)
ISBN: 978-1-63592-511-1 (pb)
ISBN: 978-1-62979-747-2 (eBook)
Library of Congress Control Number: 2016932155

First paperback edition, 2021

10 9 8 7 6 5 4 3 2 1

Design by Barbara Grzeslo
The text is set in Bembo.

For Deborah Taylor
and all librarians
who labor on behalf of
our children

Contents

It Figures 1

Origami 2

Angie 3

Summer Lost and Found 4

Stars 5

Sci-Fi Novel 6

Mom Speaks 7

Antidote 8

Rhymes with Harvey 9

Unique 10

Portrait 11

Perfect 12

Joe 13

Best Friend 14

Knock-Knock 15

Me and Joe 16

Alien 17

Tuesday 18

Phone Call 19

Dance with My Father 20

Saturday Play 21

In the Next Room 22

Sunday Dinner 23

September 24

Checkmate...25

Dressing for School 26

Day One..27

Too-Skinny-for-Words............................28

Day Two...29

Foiled...30

Second Period...31

Short Week 32

Dinner..33

Drop In..34

Shoulder-Pad Season 35

Late-Night Snack....................................36

Shadow...37

Diet 38

Stealthy Dresser 39

Secret...40

Fun Run 41

Limits...42

A Slice of Truth.......................................43

Photo Album...44

Luther's Sad Song, Again........................45

Morning Classes......................................46

Who Says?..47

Second Thoughts.....................................48

Fear 49

Turtle 50

Busted 51

Shift 52

Getting in the Groove 53

Garvey's Choice 54

Lighter than Air 55

Pact 56

First Warm-Ups 57

Chorus Calamity 58

Emmanuel 59

Saturday Catch-up 60

It's Manny, Now 61

No Words Needed 62

Careful, Now 63

Eliana 64

Where'd That Come From? 65

Advice 66

His Words 67

Come to Think of It 68

Name Game 69

Perks 70

Weekend Wonder: Manny's Spicy
        Portobello Burger Supreme 71

Rehearsal 72

Three Bears 73

Natasha Bedingfield Sings My Song 74

When I Sing 75

A Spoonful of Song 76

High School Half Day 77

Announcement 78

Manny's Turn to be Brave 79

Practice 80

Word Web 81

Preparation 82

Scales 83

The Change Bell 84

Insult 85

Good Company 86

Facing the Mirror 87

Assembly 88

Let Down 90

Thanks for the Push 91

Aftermath 92

New Fan 93

Compliments 94

Less than Perfect 95

Introductions 96

Too Soon Good-bye 97
On the Move 98
Spring Thaw 99
Colors 100
Turn Around 101
Now It's My Turn 102
First Contact 103
The Talk 104
Summer Duet 105

Tanka 107
Acknowledgments 108

It Figures

When I was seven
and crazy for Mr. Spock,
a *Star Trek* lunch box
was all I craved. Instead, Dad
bought one blaring the logo

of some football team
I'd never even heard of.
I shoved that thing in
the coal black of my closet,
then celebrated with cake.

ORIGAMI

Mom's got a talent
for origami, but she
can't fold me into
the jock Dad wants me to be.
At least, she knows not to try.

ANGIE

Angie's the athlete.
Why should I compete with her?
"Why can't Garvey be
like his sister?" I heard Dad
ask when I was eight. Mom said,

"That's the wrong question.
Ask Garvey what interests *him*.
Talk to him, honey."
Yeah, Dad, I thought. *Talk to me.*
But will he? I wish I knew.

Summer Lost and Found

Stories are breadcrumbs.
Just follow the trail of books
and you will find me
lost among the galaxies
of scorched stars and ships to Mars.

STARS

Stars on my ceiling
wink at me when the full moon
comes for a visit.
I might return the favor
someday, at least in my dreams.

For now, I strap on
chapter four of *Mars Rescue*,
study the console,
then ease back on the throttle
for a smooth flight through star fields.

SCI-FI NOVEL

On page 59,
I meet two red Martian Trills
and feel a sweet chill
ripple through me, till Dad says,
"Football would do you better."

Where did he come from?
The sudden slap of words sends
my Trills scattering.
I snarl and pound my pillow.
It's too late to slam the door.

MOM SPEAKS

Later, Mom asks him,
"Why don't you let Garvey be?"
I hear Dad snort. Twice.
"Why can't he put those books down,
play football or basketball?"

"Garvey likes to read.
When was that not a good thing?"
"Thanks, Mom," I whisper.
"You're right," says Dad. "But reading
doesn't build muscles, does it?

When I was his age,
my pop and I always played.
We roughhoused like, well—normal."
I go downstairs, grab a Coke,
wash down Dad's disappointment.

ANTIDOTE

Dinner-table talk
is magically washed away
on a sea of song
the minute I clamp on my
trusty earphones and push PLAY.

Rhymes with Harvey

Some people wonder:
Why Garvey? Why not Marcus?
So I asked my dad.
"Lots of boys named Marcus, son.
Garvey? *That's* one of a kind."

UNIQUE

How good is different?
I search stories for someone
who resembles me.
If it weren't for books and Joe,
"different" would just be lonely.

PORTRAIT

In Angela's eyes,
I'm little baby brother.
I tell her, "You're not
as much older as you think."
She spatters me with laughter.

PERFECT

Mom says I'm perfect.
Dad says I'm football-ready,
whatever that means.
Angela calls me Sweet Chunk.
"But I still love you," she says.

JOE

Joe caught me dancing
in first grade, during recess,
out back by the slide,
alone—or so I thought, till
Joe showed up and joined right in.

Seems funny now, 'cause
there was no music playing
and neither of us
minded or needed any.
We were our own melody.

We went back to class,
each waiting for the other
to spill his secret
for a laugh. But we didn't.
That's how we knew we'd be friends.

Best Friend

I like Joe's Garvey:
clever on the pitcher's mound,
wicked-smart in math,
number one at knock-knock jokes.
Do friends make better mirrors?

Knock-Knock

Here's Joe's knock–knock joke:
Joe: "Knock, knock." I say, "Who's there?"
"Orange." "Orange who?"
"Orange you going to ask
me in?" I laugh every time.

Mine's better: "Knock, knock."
"Who's there?" "Orange." "Orange who?"
"Wait. Knock, knock." "Who's there?"
"Banana." "Banana who?"
"Orange you dying to know!"

ME AND JOE

With window cracked wide,
we telescope the night sky
trailing Orion,
dreaming of supernovas,
mapping the stars for hours.

ALIEN

Over breakfast, Dad
eyes me like an alien
never seen before.
Sometimes, I could swear that he's
hoping to make first contact.

TUESDAY

Excitement beaming
from Dad's face, he bounces in,
palms a basketball.
"Look what I got for you, son!
Want to go work up a sweat?"

Who's he talking to?
After all these years, you'd think
he'd start to know me.
Will he ever stop trying
to make me someone I'm not?

PHONE CALL

All evening long, I
try tucking in my sadness,
but it keeps getting
snagged on my voice when I speak.
Joe catches it when he calls.

"Hey! What's up?" Joe asks.
Should I tell him? "Nothing you
haven't heard before.
I wish my dad could see me.
That sounds crazy, huh?"

"Not really," says Joe.
"I get it. Seriously.
But you've *got* a dad.
Mine skipped out long time ago."
Why'd I open my big mouth?

Joe shrugs off his hurt.
"Knock, knock!" he says. "Not now, Joe."
"Come on, man! Knock, knock."
I give in. "Who's there?" "Your friend,
Joe, who's always here for you."

DANCE WITH MY FATHER

"Dance with My Father"
spins on the CD player
on my dad's nightstand.
The words seep into me, then
leave my cheeks wet and salty.

SATURDAY PLAY

Soccer games display
Angela's acrobatics
out on the field, but
there's another game she plays
that we both call Distraction,

and it goes like this:
Dad juggles his ball like a
hot potato, asks,
"Who's up for running passes?"
Angela always rises.

"I could probably
use some extra exercise."
She winks at me—sign
of our conspiracy. Score!
I slip away, unnoticed.

IN THE NEXT ROOM

Mom gets her chess set,
teaches me about
bishops, knights, pawns, then
says, "Football is fine, but this
is exercise for your brain!"

SUNDAY DINNER

Joe and I stretch the
afternoon practicing chess
long enough to skip
potato-peeling duty.
We save our strength for eating

and being grateful
for roast chicken (at my house)
and glazed ham (at his)
plus mashed potatoes that make
our mouths two caverns of joy.

An extra helping
of Mom's famous peach cobbler
earns me a death glare
from guess who? "I've worked it out,"
says Dad. "Garvey stuffs himself

so he's too slow to
run passes with his old man."
"Sure, Dad. Whatever."
That's all kinds of crazy, right?
Maybe I just love cobbler.

September

I'm on school countdown.
Bring it on! More days with Joe
and fewer with Dad
who's still mad I didn't spend break
practicing serpentine runs.

CHECKMATE

Turns out, Mom was right.
My brain's beginning to bulge
with brand new muscles.
From now on, for Joe and me,
it's chess—and astronomy.

DRESSING FOR SCHOOL

I lace up new kicks,
smile showing up like hope till
ugly whispers from
last year echo in memory,
scraping that smile from my lips.

DAY ONE

I'm armed with earphones—
a perfect solution, till
Principal tells me
school rules won't allow them. So,
here I go, nervous, naked.

TOO-SKINNY-FOR-WORDS

Too-skinny-for-words
bumps into me on purpose.
"Oops!" he says. "Sorry.
It's kinda hard to squeeze by
since you take up so much space."

Under the stairwell,
I take a beat, close my eyes,
and hum loud enough
to drown the ordinary
sound of meanness flung my way.

DAY TWO

My mirror throws back
reflections of a round boy
whose face looks like mine.
Who is he? And how have I
disappeared inside his skin?

I search through my shirts
for tan, brown, grey—colors that
can help me sneak past
any rough wall of words I'm
at risk of slamming into.

FOILED

I need a new plan.
Some dumb kid named Todd
tried to be hilarious.
"Hey, Garvey! See you A-Round.
Get it? A-Round!" Sheesh. Really?

SECOND PERIOD

I glare at the stairs,
bare my teeth, and start the climb.
Breathless in ten steps,
I'm late to science, again.
I've come to hate the change bell.

SHORT WEEK

Labor Day saved me.
Seriously. If this week
were one day longer,
I'd find a patch of earth and
pull it up over my head.

DINNER

My tongue does a dance
when Mom's spicy lasagna
is passed round to me.
"Leave us some, little piggy,"
says Angela with a grin.

Not every cut bleeds,
so maybe Sis doesn't know
how deep the wound goes.
A second heaping serving's
not enough to heal my hurt.

In between big bites,
I hum to the jazz playing
on the radio,
the melody soothing me,
wherever words left splinters.

DROP IN

Joe drops by for our
weekly game of chess, where we
babble on about
nothing in particular,
which can feel pretty perfect.

SHOULDER-PAD SEASON

The family gathers
for the first weekly huddle,
minus me. So what?
By kickoff, I'm knee-deep in
learning how to wrinkle time.

LATE-NIGHT SNACK

My candy stash gone,
the refrigerator howls
to my hollow stomach, "Come!"
On my way to the kitchen,
I catch Dad, eyes closed, humming.

I can't remember
the last time I heard Dad hum.
His voice shakes the ground,
deep as thunder. Not like mine.
Just one more way we're different.

SHADOW

My mom, dad, and sis
could fit inside my shadow
and—poof—disappear.
Whenever I stand near, that's
how it feels. They're all so small.

I could be smaller,
I think, *if I wanted to,*
if I really tried.
I swallow those words with a
tall glass of water, and sleep.

Diet

Breakfast is easy:
a cereal bar with nuts.
I figure that should
patch up my hungry spaces
till it's time for the apple

I brought for lunch. Wrong.
My stomach's an angry bowl
of empty. Why'd I
turn down today's menu of
juicy cheeseburgers and fries?

STEALTHY DRESSER

After a quick lunch,
I hit the boy's locker room
five minutes early,
jam on my gym uniform
so no one sees me naked.

SECRET

Someone's at the door,
Dad's old friend, guitar in hand.
He mentions "the band."
"No time," says Dad. "Have fun, though."
Me, I whisper, "Band? What band?"

I ask him later,
learn the meaning of regret.
Dad's head snaps around.
"Since when do you listen in
on private conversations?"

I thought I'd ask Mom,
but what if she went to Dad?
He'd only get mad.
So I drop it. In minutes,
the memory slips away.

FUN RUN

That's what Joe called it,
a sprint down the block and back.
I near cracked a sweat
just contemplating the run.
I huffed, puffed, and crashed halfway.

LIMITS

"You okay, buddy?"
Joe bends over me, all love.
I tuck in my shame
with my shirt, cough up a joke.
"Dang! This was easy on Mars!"

"Well," I tell myself,
"I've got some homework to do."
I stagger upstairs,
flip on something with a groove,
and sing my way into math.

A Slice of Truth

Skipped another lunch,
then piled my plate at dinner.
Might as well give up.
Lose one pound, then put on three.
Diets are not helping me.

PHOTO ALBUM

I flip through pictures
of Dad when he was my age,
laughing while Grandpa
held him in a loose headlock,
close as I wish we could be.

"What was Grandpa like?"
I ask Dad after dinner.
He shrugs. "Strong. Silent."
"Like you, then. Never talking."
"He talked some," says Dad. "Football.

Pigskin, the grid iron,
throws, passes, tackles, touchdowns—
I guess you could say
football's the way Dad and me
knew how to be together."

Here, I've been thinking
Dad pushed me to play football
'cause he thought I was
weird, or some kind of weakling.
I had it wrong, all along.

LUTHER'S SAD SONG, AGAIN

"Dance with My Father"
plays in the kitchen while I
choke on eggs, missing
my right-here dad like Luther
missed his own gone-so-long dad.

MORNING CLASSES

Blue notes, sad as me,
wail their way from a classroom
I've never been in.
"Chorus," says Joe when I ask.
"It's a new club. You should join.

You're always singing,
or at least humming out loud."
"Yeah, but I don't know."
"Look," says Joe, "your voice is choice.
You should let others hear it."

WHO SAYS?

I know some kids think
chorus is full of sissies.
"Ignore them," Joe says.
I nod my head but wonder
whether Dad will think that, too.

SECOND THOUGHTS

Chorus. The word sings.
It may not bring me closer
to my dad, but still,
chorus might be a way to
fill in the puzzle of me.

FEAR

Fear is that flip-flop
in my belly, like when I
tried out for baseball.
All I got for my trouble
was being laughed off the field.

Will this be the same?
What if I open my mouth
and out comes—nothing?
Will kids laugh me out the door?
I can't take that anymore.

TURTLE

In a week, Joe asks,
"So, have you joined chorus yet?"
I sigh, turtle in.
"May not be for me," I say.
"In other words, you're afraid."

BUSTED

Best thing about friends:
they know you inside and out.
Worst thing about friends:
they know you inside and out.
My turtle shell is useless.

SHIFT

Joe's head hangs heavy,
warning me he's got bad news.
"I switched math class, then
the school switched my lunchtime, too."
For once, I don't feel hungry.

Getting in the Groove

I groove on Luther,
whose music lives at my house.
"Love Won't Let Me Wait,"
"Endless Love," "Your Secret Love"—
How many love songs are there?

No thank you. I'll pass.
But somewhere Luther V. said
being true matters.
The words weren't in a song, but
they sound like music to me.

GARVEY'S CHOICE

Ignoring my nerves,
I march into the classroom,
squeak out why I've come.
Feeling numb, I take a breath,
tickle that first note, then soar.

My voice skips octaves
like a smooth stone on a lake.
That's what they tell me.
"Well, class," says the director.
"Guess we found our new tenor."

LIGHTER THAN AIR

I would have skipped home,
but I told myself, "Act cool."
Couldn't help the grin.
Try wiping it off my face.
Go on! I double dare you!

PACT

I float up our stairs,
breeze into Angela's room,
forgetting to knock.
My goofy grin short-circuits
her lecture on privacy.

"Okay. What is it?"
"You'll never guess," I whisper.
"I just joined chorus!"
Sis bubbles up like soda.
"Great! So why the whispering?"

"You're the only one
I can tell. Except for Joe.
Don't want Dad to know.
Or Mom, because she'd tell him."
Sis bites her locked lips and nods.

First Warm-Ups

Ask me what scales are.
Yesterday, I'd say, "fish skin."
Now, I push my voice
to climb a new kind of stair:
do, *re*, *mi* in F and G.

CHORUS CALAMITY

Paler than skim milk,
a strange boy sits next to me.
I can't help but stare.
"It's called albinism," he
says. The word makes me shiver.

My whispered "sorry"
floats on the air between us.
The pink-eyed boy shrugs.
"This is me. Get over it."
Sounds like something I should say.

EMMANUEL

Tryouts behind me,
I'm suddenly feeling brave.
"My name is Garvey,"
I tell Pink Eyes next to me.
He sizes me up, then smiles.

"Emmanuel, here,
mostly Manny to my friends."
I'm quick to accept
his casual invitation.
"Cool. Nice to meet you, Manny."

"I made a new friend,"
I tell Joe when I see him.
"Good," he says. "'Bout time
you had you another bud.
Only so much one can do!"

Joe gives me a wink,
making sure I get the joke.
He's right, though. I need
to spread my friendship around
so it won't get too heavy.

SATURDAY CATCH-UP

"Well? So how's chorus?"
asks Joe, and my words burn bright.
"Okay! First, there's scales!
You climb this mountain of sound,
and your voice reaches higher

than it's ever been—
sweet! Then we learn a new song,
And our voices meet,
and the teacher mixes these
harmonies like music stew

and it's delicious!"
"Wow!" says Joe. "So you like it?"
"You would, too," I say.
"Yeah, but I can't sing worth spit,"
says Joe. "True," I say. "Details."

It's Manny, Now

Manny sits with me
in the cafeteria,
opens his lunch box
as if it's a treasure chest,
and he expects to find gold.

Out comes a croissant
crammed with guacamole and
two kinds of cheeses
that are not American.
Manny sees me gawking. "What

are you staring at?"
"Nothing. I've just never seen
a sandwich like that."
"Mmm," Manny hums between bites.
"You don't know what you're missing.

Here. You want a taste?"
he asks, breaking off a piece.
"I made it myself."
I chew on Gouda and this:
Manny wants to be a chef!

NO WORDS NEEDED

Manny says his dad
thinks that cooking is for girls.
"He doesn't get me,"
moans Manny. I reach over,
squeeze my new brother's shoulder.

CAREFUL, NOW

"How's your new friend?" asks
Joe. I don't want him thinking
Manny takes his place,
so I wrap my answer in
words dull as dust. "He's okay."

Joe presses for more.
"Well, what's he like, exactly?"
I give him a shrug.
"He's smart, easy to talk to—
but he can't play chess like you!"

ELIANA

School lunch is a treat
now that Manny brings extra
eats to share with me.
He says he gets ideas from
some kid named Eliana,

a kid who's a chef!
Is that even possible?
Manny serves up a
cold dish of truth: a cookbook
with her name on the cover!

Eliana Cooks!
Recipes for Creative
Kids. "This will be me,"
says Manny. "One day. Just wait."
I smile, tasting his success.

WHERE'D THAT COME FROM?

The change bell always
sinks fear into me like teeth.
Ugly name-calling
leaves me with bloody bite marks:
lard butt, fatso, Mister Tubs.

"Your mama!" rests on
the tip of my tongue, today,
though I don't say it.
But when I hear, "Yo, Two-Ton!"
the words, "Yo, No-Brain!" slip out.

ADVICE

Later, when chorus
is done, I hang with Manny,
join him on the bus.
"Got something on your mind, G?"
I like when he calls me that.

"I was wondering
how you stand kids teasing you."
"I'm honest," he says.
"I've got albinism. Fact.
I look strange. No changing that.

Is there more to me?
Sure. Kids yell 'albino boy.'
I don't turn around.
Choose the name you answer to.
No one can do that but you."

HIS WORDS

Manny tells me he
was made in God's own image.
"God is beautiful,"
he says. "So what's that make you
and me? Do you get it, G?"

I carry his words
in the pocket of my mind.
A few times a day,
they remind me to ignore
the kids who don't know my name.

Come to Think of It

Why let Angela
call me something that I'm not?
Or let her tease me?
Bad enough the kids at school
kick my heart around for fun.

NAME GAME

Sis falls through the door,
juggles backpack and groceries.
"Hey there, Chocolate Chunk.
"How 'bout giving me a hand?"
Call me that one more time and . . .

The terrible sound
of teeth grinding fills my ears.
Tears aren't far behind.
I bite my lip and whisper,
"My name is Garvey. Got it?"

Angela withers.
"I'm sorry, Garvey," she says.
"I was just teasing."
"Yeah? So why am I bleeding?"
Pow! Maybe she gets it now.

Perks

Manny waves to me
'cross the cafeteria.
I pocket my coins.
Sharing Manny's scrumptious lunch
means more money for music!

WEEKEND WONDER: MANNY'S SPICY PORTOBELLO BURGER SUPREME

Grilled portobello
with roasted peppers, onions,
sliced jalapeños,
topped with melted Havarti
makes my taste buds want to dance.

REHEARSAL

I count the hours
until chorus meets again.
Now "fat boy" insults
glide right off me like raindrops.
I dance in the pool they make.

THREE BEARS

It doesn't matter
how wide I am when I sing.
Like Goldilocks, I
have finally found what fits:
my high tenor is just right.

NATASHA BEDINGFIELD SINGS MY SONG

I'm just beginning
to learn what I am made of,
to pay attention
to the kid in my own eyes,
starting to like what I see.

I feel unwritten
like that song says, in chorus,
my story untold.
I can't wait to sing the song,
croon my own untold story.

WHEN I SING

When I sing, my heart
floats full and light, as if I'm
a balloon of song,
rising with every lyric,
reaching the edges of space.

A Spoonful of Song

My chocolate stash
is lasting me much longer.
These days, nothing tastes
sweet as four-part harmony.
Somehow, music makes me full.

High School Half Day

Angela crashes
chorus practice, hears me sing.
After my solo,
her eyes are wet pools of pride.
"Dad needs to hear you, Garvey.

You. Have. To. Tell. Him."
Angela insists. Her words
grind my doubt to dust.
She's right. This isn't football,
but here, I'm the quarterback.

ANNOUNCEMENT

That night, I announce
that I sing in the chorus,
have my own solo,
say it like it's no big deal,
then leap inside when Dad smiles.

MANNY'S TURN TO BE BRAVE

"You should audition
for that television show:
MasterChef Junior."
"Yeah?" asks Manny. "I don't know."
He shrugs, so I let it go.

PRACTICE

"Practice makes perfect,"
the chorus teacher tells me.
My voice won't listen.
Why can't I hit the high note?
I sigh, start the song again.

WORD WEB

I fall into bed,
Have Space Suit—Will Travel propped
up on my nightstand.
Read? Sleep? The story spools out
spider silk and captures me.

PREPARATION

Our first recital!
Dad proudly takes me shopping
for a brand new suit.
Just wait until he hears me
split the air with waves of song!

"You know, Son," Dad says,
"I used to sing solo, too—
a long time ago."
His words stir memory: an
old friend, whispers of a band . . .

SCALES

Each night, I run scales,
looking into my mirror,
making sure my mouth
matches the shapes teacher taught.
Who knew singing could be work?

The Change Bell

I do like Manny,
crank up the inside volume,
listen to my dreams
as I walk through the school halls.
I choose what words to let in.

INSULT

Leaving rehearsal,
word bombs explode behind me:
a girl yells "Dump Truck,"
trying to shatter my joy.
I almost let her. Almost.

GOOD COMPANY

I'm missing Joe, but
I escape a lonely lunch
'cause Manny joins me.
"There goes Garvey and the Ghost!"
some kids tease, but I like it.

We talk between bites.
Me: "Wish I could wake up thin."
Manny: "My mom says,
'Shine your light, no one will care
what size candle holds the flame.'

Take your man, Luther.
I've almost never heard folks
laugh about his weight.
I've just heard them praising him
for his smooth-as-velvet voice."

I chew on his words,
wash them down with chocolate milk.
Maybe someday I'll
lift my voice to the heavens
and have praise rain down on me.

FACING THE MIRROR

My waist a stranger
I haven't seen in ages,
I grit my teeth, speak
the truth: My body's chunky.
Who cares? It's just the spaceship

the real me rides in.
Right? So I dress for the day,
give my cap a tilt,
and fire up the engines,
set to face a new morning.

ASSEMBLY

Single file, we march
on stage for our recital.
Louder than a zoo,
the kids watching point and laugh,
hyenas in human skin.

Teachers hiss and shush,
quieting the animals
until they become
an audience of students
squirming in their seats and bored.

Like water ripples,
our first notes spread harmony
from front row to back.
I see my classmates floating
in sound, and I stand taller.

Manny nudges me
when it's time for my solo.
Legs like spaghetti,
I worry that I might faint.
Eyes closed, I wait for courage.

A whisper at first,
the music in me rises.
Live inside the song,
I tell myself. And I do.
Then comes the hush, and applause.

LET DOWN

During the applause,
I search for him in the crowd,
catch him with head bowed,
cringe, certain I've failed again
till I see Dad wipe his eyes.

THANKS FOR THE PUSH

Like hard candy, "thanks"
sticks in my throat, melts slowly.
Waiting for the words,
I jab Manny in the arm,
mimicking movie tough guys.

AFTERMATH

Sis bounces up, flings
an arm across my shoulder,
staking out her claim.
"This is my brother, Garvey,"
she says, leaving me speechless.

NEW FAN

Dad stands to the side
beaming pride like a nova,
lighting up my year.
Mom's crushing hugs, expected.
The nod from Dad, like Christmas.

COMPLIMENTS

Joe comes—no surprise—
pats me on the back. "Garvey!
My man, you killed it!"
The stars 'round Mars have nothing
on me, tonight. I shine bright.

"Kid, you got some pipes."
This from Too-skinny-for-words!
I watch his eyes turn
an envy green, a color
I have never seen him wear.

Less than Perfect

Grim shadows, problems
haunt us all—round, thin, short, tall.
Too-skinny-for-words
is unhappy to the core.
Never noticed that before.

INTRODUCTIONS

I end the evening
sandwiched between my best friends.
"Joe, this is Manny."
"I've been hearing about you,"
both begin in unison,
then we three drown in laughter.

Too Soon Good-bye

Luther died before
I knew his music, his name.
It's the why of it
makes me want to punch a wall.
He shouldn't have died at all.

News stories agree.
What did him in was his weight,
all that yo-yoing
up and down, losing, gaining.
His heart just couldn't take it.

I did the right thing,
giving up crash dieting.
Maybe it's better
to eat less, jog with Joe, go
slow so I can stick around.

ON THE MOVE

I show up at Joe's,
sporting brand-new running shoes.
Once he stops laughing,
Joe joins me for my first jog.
One block and I am wheezing.

Soon, each morning finds
the two of us out jogging
twice around the block.
Sometimes, Joe asks, "Are you good?"
To answer, I run faster!

Sometimes when I run,
I feel Dad's eyes follow me.
He won't admit it,
but when I come in sweaty,
he always gives me a nod.

SPRING THAW

Peeled myself from bed
for the morning rush to school.
(Better beat the bell!)
Belted a blue-jean surprise:
loose waist by nearly one size!

Round still, but that's fine.
Feeling good outside and in.
Maybe I'm not thin,
but skinny isn't perfect.
The perfect size is happy.

Colors

My shirt red as flame,
I stand before the mirror,
smiling at a boy
whose frame is familiar
but changed, unfinished—all me.

TURN AROUND

At lunch, Manny says,
"Looks like your dad came around."
"Yes!" the word explodes
from my chest. "Think mine can, too,
if I do that TV show?"

This time, I chew on
hope for my good friend. "Manny,
you're ready for this!
Win or lose, your dad will see
that real men can be great chefs."

NOW IT'S MY TURN

Next week, I shop for
encouragement: *Cool Kids Cook:*
Fresh & Fit, a book
by Kid Chef Eliana,
a small gift to lift a friend.

FIRST CONTACT

A knock at my door.
It's Dad, a CD in hand.
"Say, have you heard this
album? The title track is
Luther's best—and my favorite."

Dance with My Father!
Something warm rises in me.
I'd speak if I could.
Instead, I give Dad the smile
I've been saving forever.

THE TALK

"Son, I should tell you,
I used to sing in a band,"
Dad says in the voice
he saves for secrets. I smile,
and pretend that I'm surprised.

"Really? When?" I ask.
"Oh, it was a long while back . . ."
That's how it began—
the longest conversation
I've ever had with my dad.

SUMMER DUET

Dad's old band tunes up
at our house on Saturdays.
You should hear how his
bluesy bass rhythms rock my
high-tenor melodies—sweet!

TANKA

Tanka is an ancient poetry form, originally from Japan. The word *tanka* means "short poem" in Japanese. The basic tanka is five lines long. The line-by-line syllable count varies in the modern English version, but the number of lines is always the same.

The modern form of tanka I chose to use for *Garvey's Choice* is broken down as follows:

Line 1: 5 syllables
Line 2: 7 syllables
Line 3: 5 syllables
Line 4: 7 syllables
Line 5: 7 syllables.

Not every American poet follows a syllable count for tanka poems, but I think of a syllable count like a puzzle. Each word is a puzzle piece, and I like figuring out which words fit best!

Traditional tanka poems focus on mood. They are often poems about love, the four seasons, the shortness of life, and nature. In my tanka, I include mood, but in each poem, my focus is more centered on telling a story.

I hope you enjoyed the stories I told!

ACKNOWLEDGMENTS

Throughout the journey of every book, there are book-angels to thank, those good souls who nudge the work along with encouragement, critique, cajoling, and infusions of decadent dark chocolate, as needed. *Garvey's Choice* is no exception.

I have to thank Jane Yolen for hosting me for a writing retreat at her home, during which time I struggled through an early draft of this novel in the restful environment of her studio. Thank you for your hospitality, not to mention treating me to the Eric Carle and the Emily Dickinson museums! Jane, you are a kind and generous friend.

Thanks also to Han Nolan and her husband, Brian, who hosted me for a second writing retreat, during which time I nailed down the final major draft of this book. Han, your insightful critique helped to set me up for success! I'm grateful for your friendship.

Finally, thanks to my intrepid editor, Rebecca Davis. You're always willing to duke it out with me, in the interest of producing the best book possible. I wouldn't trade you for the world.

Here's hoping this much-cared-for book finds its audience!

GARVEY'S CHOICE
THE GRAPHIC NOVEL

By Nikki Grimes
Illustrated by Theodore Taylor III

Photograph by Sarah Schultz-Taylor

Theodore Taylor III is the illustrator of multiple books, including *When the Beat Was Born,* for which he received the Coretta Scott King John Steptoe New Talent Award. He lives in Richmond, Virginia, with his wife and son. Visit theodore3.com.

DISCOVER NIKKI GRIMES'S
WORDS WITH WINGS

Gabby has been a daydreamer for as long as she can remember, but when her parents began arguing, daydreaming became as essential as breathing. At first an escape, it's now taken over her life. Will Gabby ever find a way to keep her thoughts grounded? Or could her daydreams help her take flight?

PRAISE AND HONORS FOR *WORDS WITH WINGS*

Coretta Scott King Author Honor Book
An ALSC Notable Children's Book
A Kirkus Reviews Best Children's Book of the Year

★ *Kirkus Reviews*, starred review
★ *Booklist*, starred review

Garvey loves astronomy, science fiction, chess, and music. But it's through music that he gains confidence, and he muses that "chorus might be a way to fill in the puzzle of me." When developing Garvey's character, did you intentionally choose these four subjects because they're interrelated somehow? Are these things you love as well?

I gave only a passing thought to the way astronomy and science fiction were related. I knew that Garvey was a reader, and it only made sense that his love of the stars would be reflected in his choice of books. Music was the key to connect Garvey and his dad, of course. As for chess, it provided a way for Garvey's mother to highlight her son's intellectual capacity and, in the process, counter some of the father's negative messages about Garvey's perceived lack of athletic skills.

And, yes, I have an appreciation for all four subjects, myself, though not to an equal degree. My father was a violinist and composer, and so I come by my love of music naturally. I enjoy science fiction and have read the occasional sci-fi novel. I'm fascinated by the solar system, and I admire anyone who can play chess!

Garvey and Manny both struggle because the things that they're passionate about—singing and cooking— are not considered manly activities by significant

**adults in their lives. How important is it to pursue
your dreams even if doing so will make you stand
out for being different?**

No matter what anyone says or thinks about your dreams,
you must always pursue them. Usually, when you're
successful, the naysayers come around. But even if they don't,
you owe it to yourself to follow your heart and to make use
of whatever gifts you were given. The talents God gave you
are your gifts to the world.

**Manny and Garvey are often the objects of bullying
in school, and Manny's response to his albinism gives
Garvey courage to defend himself. What would you
tell kids who witness someone being bullied?**

Stand up for kids who are being bullied. No one deserves to
be bullied, but unless someone stands up for that person, the
victim might start to believe that he or she does deserve it,
and that would be a shame.

**Garvey loves food and is overweight partly because
he uses it for comfort. Did you, from the beginning,
plan for Manny to dream of being a chef in order to
give Garvey different ways of thinking about food?
Or did this unfold as you developed your characters?**

So much of what happens in a novel is surprising, and
organic. I had no idea Manny would harbor dreams of being
a chef. I wanted Manny to have a passion of his own, though,
and I'm not surprised my mind went in this direction. I'm
obsessed with cooking shows. In addition, I have a friend

whose teen daughter, Eliana, is a rising star in the culinary world, so the notion of a young person dreaming of a career as a chef wasn't much of a leap for me. That Manny's passion allowed me to explore ways Garvey might wake up to the idea of healthy eating, and food as fuel, rather than comfort, was a bonus.

You chose to tell Garvey's story in tanka poems. What made you want to write a whole novel using one poetic form? What do you like about tankas?

The novel actually grew out of a question I asked myself, one day. I wondered if it was possible to write a novel entirely in tanka poems. The first draft of this novel was my attempt to do so.

I always like to challenge myself, to push my boundaries as an artist and writer. There's something about inherent limits of a tightly structured form like tanka that draws me to it. I wanted to look for ways to bend it to my use, to force emotional truth within the limits of those five lines—a nearly impossible task, which is what made it irresistible to me. I simply had to give it a try.

New York Times best-selling author Nikki Grimes is the recipient of the ALAN Award for outstanding contributions to young adult literature, the Children's Literature Legacy Award, the Virginia Hamilton Literary Award, and the NCTE Award for Excellence in Poetry for Children. Her distinguished works include the Coretta Scott King Award-winner *Bronx Masquerade* and five Coretta Scott King Author Honor books—*Words with Wings*, *The Road to Paris*, *Dark Sons*, *Jazmin's Notebook*, and *Talkin' About Bessie*. Her memoir *Ordinary Hazards* won a Boston Globe-Horn Book Nonfiction Honor Award, a Michael L. Printz Honor Award for Excellence in Young Adult Literature, a Robert F. Sibert Informational Book Honor Award, and the Arnold Adoff Poetry Award for Teens. Ms. Grimes lives in Corona, California. Visit nikkigrimes.com.